Christmas Love and Miracles

By
Ruth Bawell

Table of Contents

Unsolicited Testimonials............. 4

FREE GIFT......................... 5

Chapter One..................... 6

Chapter Two.................. 25

Chapter Three............... 43

Chapter Four............... 82

Chapter Five.............. 97

FREE GIFT................. 113

Please Check out My Other Works..... 114

Thank You.................. 115

Unsolicited Testimonials

By **Phyllis**

★★★★★ **Love Ruth!**

I love Ruth's books! Her mysteries are the best!

★★★★★ **Love This Author**

Ruth Bawell is very creative and a great writer! All her books have left me unable to stop reading till the ending! There were a few Amish fact mistakes, like unmarried man having a beard, but the plot was so good I overlooked that!

By **Steve M**

★★★★★ **I love romance stories** August 5, 2017
I love romance stories... well written with her usual twists to the story still enjoyed them very much Once I start I can't put it down.

By **Bones**

★★★★★ **Amish County Stories**
I love all the Amish County stories! Each one brings so much excitement! Ruth Bawell is also a wonderful writer!

By **Kindle Customer**

★★★★★ **Good clean writing.**
The Amish stories of Ruth Bawell are authentic, faith-filled writings. They are short, more the length of novellas or longer short stories. Always clean, always uplifting.

Chapter One

The horse galloped along the county road, pulling behind the single bench buggy controlled by a driver. In the back sat Manuel Zook, looking out from the small window, taking in the scenery. The sight of it filled him with nostalgic feelings. Manuel felt a little forlorn as they journeyed into the town, bidding goodbyes to the city behind them.

It had been years since he last saw his hometown. He had left home three years earlier to live with his uncle in a community in the next state. There he had worked on his uncle's orchard farm while helping his uncle, who at the time was bereaved and needed comfort and assistance.

The family had sent Manuel off to keep the old man company. His uncle was very kind and understanding, and Manuel was teachable and supportive. Hence the two got along quite well, and after the passing of a couple of years, they had grown the orchard into one of the biggest and most productive ones around town.

Now, Manuel was heading home to spend the Christmas holidays with his family for the first time in three years. Although he wrote them every month and received letters from home too, he missed them and wondered what they looked like now.

On what used to be only bare lands and farmlands three years ago when he left town now stood many houses scattered around with gardens and barnyards. The whole village felt and looked different, only better. They passed by a few fields where men and women were harvesting and gathering the last of the dried hay to store in the barns.

The buggy driver began to hum a tune as he swayed his head from side to side. It was one of those familiar hymns Manuel knew by heart from childhood. He smiled as he remembered how his family and a few neighboring family friends would gather in groups for days leading up to the celebration to make arrangements for Christmas day. There would be lots of food and baked goodies to prepare, and their house would sometimes be decorated with homemade sweet-smelling vanilla and lavender candlesticks. Later in the evening, they would sit together in a large circle, singing mellifluous tunes, the special Christmas celebration hymns.

The winter weather was quite frosty today. Manuel had worn the woolen sweater and gloves his mamm had handmade specially for him as a gift to remind him of home some days before he left town. He hugged it a bit tighter this evening. It smelt so much like home. So much like his mamm's hug. He had missed her so much, and no amount of written words could suffice.

Apart from his mom and family, Manuel longed to meet someone else once again; one of his childhood best friends. Abigail, with whom he had shared most of his fondest childhood memories, from their one-room classroom to singing together at the farmhouse gatherings, to running around on the fields on bright autumn days, to picking earthworms together in their family gardens and playing board games in the evenings and all the memorable moments they enjoyed in the company of their families.

The two families were close associates, and so their friendship blossomed naturally. Often, their siblings would make jokes that they would fall in love eventually and get married, but they never got around to it.

For Manuel, Abigail had always been more than a friend since they were seven, but he was afraid that he was nothing more than that to her. As a result, his feelings remained unrequited because he never actually expressed them to Abigail out of fear that she might reject his advances.

Although they had remained cordial through the years, they had somehow grown apart as teenagers as they began to search for new interests and make new friends outside their group.

At twenty-one, Manuel felt it was about time he got a frau and settle down to build a home as many of the young men his age were about to do. There was no other person he could think of as a more suitable life partner for him than Abigail. He needed a nice young Amish woman with strong values and Christian qualities like Abigail to complement him. Now going back home, Manuel hoped he would find the courage to communicate his feelings for her. They shared so much in common and would make a great couple.

"Where is your stop, young man?" the driver asked, jostling Manuel back to reality.

"Down the end of the road, sir," he responded, pointing ahead in the direction.

The driver nudged the reins of the horse, which caused the animal to gallop a little faster.

"Are you visiting?" the man asked, turning to steal a glance at the passenger in the back.

"Yes, sir. I've come to spend the Christmas celebration with my family," Manuel responded.

"Have you been away for very long?"

"It's been three years now."

"You must miss your folks then," the old driver said, sighing.

"I miss them a whole lot. I can't wait to see all of them again."

"You sure do. I also remember a time in my youth when I had left home to learn work in town," the man recalled.

The horse came to a halt in the front where a large, two-story farmhouse backed by a few stands of trees with bared branches stood. Manual folded back the wagon blanket he had used to shield himself from the cold breeze that penetrated the doors and pulled on some gloves and a coat before he stepped out of the buggy. He thanked the man and paid his fare.

"Merry Christmas in advance," the driver said before he circled off.

"Merry Christmas," Manuel greeted even as the man was out of earshot.

As he stood in front of his house, a rush of emotions swarmed through him. Scenes from his wonderful times in this house flickered through his mind. A thick layer of powdery fresh snow muffled his footsteps as he walked across the path over to his front porch. Before he could step onto the front porch, the door flung open and his sister appeared, jumping into his arms.

"Manny," she cried out in delight.

"Adah. My goodness, you have grown so big," he exclaimed as he almost lost his footing and managed to regain his composure.

"I could say the same about you, bruder. You hardly look the same. Welcome home," Adah announced as she collected his luggage off his hands and proceeded to lead him into the house, with Manuel following behind. "Mamm has been waiting the whole day for you. She wouldn't leave the house. You know Mamm. She insisted on giving you a feast for a welcome. If she had her way, she would throw a town celebration on your behalf."

Manuel smiled knowingly. He pulled off his coat and shook the snow off before handing it to his sister. Before he could take off his gloves, his mamm appeared from her room and came down the stairs in fast strides. Immediately, mamm and son launched towards each other and threw their arms together in a warm embrace.

"Gott be praised. My son is home," his mamm proclaimed as she pulled back and cast a studying glance at him. Then she cupped his face into her hands and pulled him back into her embrace again. "We have missed you so much, son," she said.

"I have missed you too, mama," Manny replied, his eyes watering just a little bit from the outburst of overwhelming emotions.

"We always looked forward to your letters every month. We would all read them sitting together in the evenings as if they were storytelling books," his little bruder said as he crouched over to hug him.

One by one, all five of his siblings came over to welcome him. He brought out some candies from his bag for the younger children.

"Where is Father?" Manuel asked, darting his eyes around the room. Apart from a few visible refurbishments done in the house, everywhere still looked and felt the same.

"Your father went for a meeting with some of the elders," his mamm said.

"But he's been gone for the past couple of hours now, so we expect him to be back any time soon," his sister, Jael, added.

"How is your uncle? Is he well now? Your last letter where you mentioned his health problem was a little cause of concern for your father. You know how much he worries about his bruder since his loss," Frau Gaius inquired, a frown burrowing out on her forehead.

"He's alright, mama. He was a bit unwell recently due to stress from work on the farm. Still, I was able to get him a doctor to visit regularly and a maid to assist him around the house before I took my leave. He sent his greetings," he announced as he waved at everyone in the room.

"You have done so well, son. Your father will be so proud of you. Now hurry, go up to your room and freshen up. Your father should be back any minute so we can have supper together."

Manuel began up the staircase. He could still remember which one was his room. He stopped in the corridor and looked around for a moment before he pushed open the door and stepped into the room. The room was almost the way he left it; the only difference was that it had been cleaned spotless and brushed to perfection. The air in the room was cozy and smelled of lavender. His mamm must have ensured it was freshened up with his favorite homemade fragrances.

It was very warm here, unlike the cold weather outside. By the wall was a large stove burning with hot coals to keep the room heated at all times. There was one of such in every room. It was how their mamm made sure their rooms were warm enough in the winters.

The bed was well stocked up with bundles of quilts for adequate warming. He walked over to the window and gazed outside. The evening fog was gently rising, and the distant woods overlooking the house were becoming hazy. Manuel sat down and felt the warm bed with his hands. He realized how much he had missed home. He let himself get emotional and said a little prayer, thanking Gott for reuniting him with his family.

From a young age, Manuel had been taught to appreciate and acknowledge the place of Gott in his life. Christmas time was always the perfect season to express his gratitude to Him for the gift of family and life. By the time he came down the stairs again, having washed up and changed his clothes, the dining table was set, and mounds of food were ready. It was as though there was a feast.

"Mama, it's not Christmas day today, is it?"

Everyone in the kitchen laughed.

"No, son. This is all for you. I know you have missed my cooking, so I took the time to make every one of your favorites," she said, gesturing at the different dishes on the table. "Come sit. You look skinny to me. Doesn't he?" She turned around, soliciting the other children to agree with her. They nodded in agreement, laughing as his mamm felt his skin to prove her point.

"Mamm, I hope you're not planning to stuff me up with all the food in this house?"

Manuel smiled. He knew how much his mamm loved to cook, and as today was somewhat special, he knew she had poured her heart into it. They all sat down at the table, and as his father was unavoidably absent, they decided to proceed without him on account of Manuel.

Manuel took a loaf of bread and spread some pear butter over it. He had missed his mamm's homemade meals so much. He took a bite and savored the taste of it.

"Hmm!" he muttered in between mouthfuls. "Mama, this butter tastes so good. There's a burst of flavor in every bite."

His mamm smiled at him with an impressed look on her face.

"Did you make it?" he asked, pointing at both of his sisters.

"No," they answered, resisting the urge to laugh.

Finally, his mamm said, "It was from Abigail. She makes pear butter and supplies them to all the homes in the district and the farmers' markets near us. I reckoned you would enjoy it, and you do." She beamed, pleased with herself for adding it to the menu.

"So, if you need some more jars, we'll be more than happy to order them all just for you," Adah, his sister, added with a grin.

"It's very delicious," he said, spreading butter onto his toast. Manuel's heart had skipped a bit when he heard Abigail's name at the dinner table, but he tried to keep his voice calm. "So, Aby's still in town?"

"Of course. Where else would she rather be?" his mamm asked, eyeing him.

"Is she married now?" he blurted out before he could help himself. Everyone stared at him in surprise. Manuel lowered his gaze to avoid their piercing eyes. He had not wanted to ask about her in his letters, but now he rather wished he had.

"No. She has not yet," Adah replied.

He leaned over to his bruder and whispered, "Is she courting someone?"

"Well, not that I know of," the younger child responded out loud to the hearing of all. He eyed his bruder, who smiled back mischievously.

"What?" He looked up at his sisters. "Why is everyone staring at me?"

They all burst out laughing.

Later that night, when his father returned, they all sat together in the living room while Manuel shared his experiences with life in the town, his uncle, and their successes at the orchard with his family. They, in turn, shared stories of life at home with him. They stayed up well into the night under the soft glint of lantern light on the lamp stand.

Chapter Two

Early the following morning, Manuel was awake, although still huddling under a mound of quilts his mamm had given him last night. The room was very cozy and warm, and he wished he could lie in bed all day, but he already had the day planned out. Groaning, he got up and took a hot bath his sister had prepared for him, taking his time to choose his clothes. He intended to visit Abigail and hoped to look his best.

There was a soft knock on the bedroom door.

"Who is there?" he asked, pausing from his dressing.

"It's me, Abram. Mamm asks that you come down for breakfast," his bruder responded from outside the door.

"Tell mamm I will be down soon."

A minute passed before Manuel walked down the stairs to the dining room where his family sat. His father was present and seated at the head of the table. The boys sat on the right-hand side while the women sat on the left. His empty seat was there, next to his father, as it had always been before he left home.

Breakfast was scrambled eggs, fried potatoes, bacon, bread, some biscuits, and pear butter which Manuel had already grown a liking for. Father said a prayer, and they all chorused an "Amen."

Breakfast was eaten amidst chatters as they all shared their itineraries for the day.

Manuel borrowed one of his father's buggies and went into the district to meet and greet some family relations and friends he had missed for so long. He visited a few of his old friends and spent some time with them. Everyone was thrilled to see him back home after such a long time.

Finally, he decided to go over to Abigail's house. He was feeling rather anxious by the time he got to their driveway, laced on each side with beautiful garden flowers.

Abigail's mamm answered the door when he knocked. She was surprised to find who it was. After they exchanged greetings, Manuel asked about Abigail and her twin bruder, Jared.

"Abigail had gone to work to pick up some pears for her next batch of butter," her mamm said. He thanked her and promised to come by some other time when everyone would be home.

Manuel got back into his buggy, driving to the place where her mamm promised he would find Abigail. He went over a mile on the boulevard, passing by the school they had attended as children. The school was just as he remembered it and probably one of the things that stayed the same over the years.

At the orchard, he found Abigail crouched over, sorting and picking some pears into a sack. Her apron hung loosely over her plain blue gown and her bonnet was firmly pinned above her bun. He stood at a distance and watched her work, trying to choose the first words he'd say to her.

***

Abigail felt a presence hovering over her. She turned around to see who it was and was startled upon putting a face to the figure behind her.

"How long have you been standing over there?" she asked, beaming with a smile and crinkling her eyes closed in disbelief.

Manuel smiled in return, transfixed where he was rooted. It was amazing how he still felt the same way about her.

When she had turned around, Manuel had been thrown off balance. He couldn't believe this was Abigail, the same little girl he knew by heart. She was stunning, with the most perfect cheekbones he had ever seen on a woman. She had lush green eyes that flickered beautifully as she spoke. Now she was in his arms, her hands wrapped tightly around him, the heat from her body sending waves of excitement cascading through his body.

She let go of him and stepped back. As their eyes met, he felt a funny kick at his heart. She had grown into a lovely woman, just as he had envisioned. He especially liked how her cheeks dimpled, and her eyes sparkled when she smiled.

"Not too long," Manuel finally responded as he took her hands, and they walked back towards the pile of pears. "I'm so pleased to see you again, Abby. You've grown into a charming woman," he said.

Abigail smiled coyly, causing the dimples to form again, sending the same quivering effect through him. They sat down on the rocks, and he offered to help Abigail sort the pears.

"I tasted some of your pear butter yesterday and this morning at home," he said as he reached over to pick a pear.

"Really?" She raised her eyes at him quizzically in a way that formed tiny wrinkles on her forehead.

"It was splendid. I almost smuggled a jar to my room last night to lick while I lay in bed."

Abigail laughed out loud when he said that.

"Well, I won't forget to give you as many jars as you might need once you're ready to leave," she joked.

"My sister already offered, but who am I to reject a wonderful gift from the Pear

Butter Mistress herself?" Manuel gushed with a smile.

They continued in silence for a few seconds. Abigail watched him as he worked effortlessly on the pears, choosing only the ripest ones to place into the sack. The young handsome Amish boy she had known all her life had matured into a tall, nice-looking man with a well-toned frame. He wore his hair short in a bowl cut style and a tidy, light-blue shirt. She was delighted that he had not changed his identity. He was still Amish and did not allow himself to stray even though he had been away from their community for so long.

"I have missed you so much," Abigail said after a while.

"I have missed you the same," Manuel replied.

"What exactly do you do over there?"

"I worked on my Uncle Sam's fruit orchard. Mostly we plant and cultivate these fruit trees from seedling to mature fruit-bearing trees. Then, we harvest the fruits and sell them to farmers. We even have pears."

"Really? That's very interesting. I would love to come to visit someday, but of course, that is not possible. I've hardly ever left the province since I was born."

"I can take you with me," Manuel said.

Abigail frowned, creasing her forehead. "I doubt you would," she deadpanned and gently shoved him.

"I'm serious, Abby. You only need to agree to come with me."

She stared at him now with a thoughtful expression, propping her chin on her hands.

"Alright. I hear you. I hope one day you'll bring back some pears for me, though."

By now, they were done sorting and gathering the pears in the sack.

"How do you transport them home?" Manuel asked.

"My bruder will be coming around by five p.m. to pick me up in his buggy."

"You mean you would have to wait here for that long? Out here all alone in the cold?" he asked with a puzzled look on his face. "Come, I'll give you a ride to the storehouse and then take you home."

"What if my bruder comes here to find me? He may get really worried."

"I'm sure we will get back to the house before he does. We might even go straight to his woodshop to inform him. How about that?"

She seemed unconvinced, and so, he tried again.

"Look. The fog is gathering and it might start to snow again soon. Let me drive you home. Your mom knows I'm here, remember? She may likely tell your bruder anyways."

She glanced up at the sky. It looked very cloudy now. She seemed to consider what he had said and finally nodded.

"Alright. Let's go."

Manuel picked up one of the sacks and strode towards the buggy. Abigail stood there watching him move and smiled to herself. Then, she started to drag the second sack through the snow-covered ground. Manuel returned to see her groaning while tugging the sack with all her might. He hid a smile as he walked over to her and grabbed the sack with one hand.

Abigail stopped, arms akimbo.

"Did you just sneer at me?" she asked, plumping her lips into a pout.

Manuel could not hold it in any longer. He burst out laughing.

"You should have seen yourself dragging that sack along. An amusing sight."

She joined him, and when they got to the buggy, Manuel slowly lowered the sack into the back and shut it tight. Then, he opened the door and offered her his hands, which she took, and helped her onto the seat.

"Denke, gentleman," she said teasingly.

"You're welcome," he nodded and smiled as he walked over to the driver's side and pulled the horse's harness. The animal began to gallop down the steep snow-covered street.

"So, how do you make the pear butter?"

"You have to clean and chop the pears into sizes and season them with some choice spices, add some water and lemon juice. Cook until the pears are completely softened. Then you turn the mixture into a strainer and strain the mixture through. Make sure you discard the remaining tough matter. Then, you pour the soft porridge into a large cooking pan with some sugar and stir until the sugar dissolves. I add the spices then and cook it until it thickens, then cool it and store it in jars," she finished breathlessly.

Manuel had listened patiently while she explained the process, careful not to interrupt her. And although he had some questions, he waited until she had finished.

"How long does the whole process last?"

"About forty minutes to two hours,"

"So how do you preserve it?"

"You'll have to put the jars back in hot water and bring them to a boil. It can last for up to a year after."

"Really?" He asked.

"Yes. It can."

"That's interesting. I reckon you must have some secret ingredients you'd like to share." He winked at her, laughing.

"Are you trying to steal my recipes? I'm never telling my secret ingredients," she responded. "Never!"

They both exchanged a friendly look and laughed cheerfully.

As they got to the storehouse, the horse pulled to a stop. Manuel stepped out of the carriage and opened the door for her. Then, he turned to the back and pulled out the sacks, careful not to damage the pears inside.

Abigail led the way to the storehouse and opened it up. Manuel carried the sack into the store and headed back for the second sack. When he returned, she locked up again, and they returned to the buggy. They drove back, making sure to stop at Abigail's bruder's woodshop to inform him that he was giving Abigail a ride home.

Jared was Abigail's twin bruder, and they all used to play together as children. The buggy stopped, and Abby opened the door first before Manuel could circle to her side of the carriage. When her bruder saw her walking towards him, he glanced at the clock on the wall.

"Abby, I was about to come to take you home soon. How did you get...?" Before Jared could finish his sentence, he saw Manuel walking behind her.

"Guess who is in town and decided to show up at the farm?" Abigail said.

"Manny!" Jared called out.

"Jared!"

The two men shook hands and collapsed in a hug.

"Wow! It's been a long time. How long? Three years?"

"Yes. Three years since I last saw your face," Manuel responded with a wide smile.

"We have missed you so much over here. I'm so happy to see you again."

"Same here."

Abigail spoke up then. "Guess what? Manuel offered to drive me home. I would have loved to ride with you if I didn't already agree to go with him," Abby said with a grin and laughed.

"That's very kind of him." Her bruder winked. "I don't mind if he decides to drive you every day; it takes the work off my hands."

"Oh. I never knew my twin was getting so tired of me," Abby said, pretending to sob. The two men laughed at her.

"No. You know I would never trade you for anything in the world, dearest sister," Jared teased gently.

Chapter Three

It was nine days to Christmas. This week's Sunday service lasted for three hours. The service was held at Herr Wheeler's home, Abigail's father. The day's sermon centered on the Christmas season as a true representation of Gott's love for man.

The barn, where the congregation gathered, was divided into two rows. All the males sat on the right row while the women sat on the left. Manuel had found a place in the back bench row, from where he could see Abigail on the other side of the congregation.

Today Abigail wore her regular Sunday dress, a plain-colored blue gown with a white apron. Her hair was tightly braided and twisted in a bun at the back of her head, with her scarf and bonnet secured on it. From the back, she didn't look much different from the rest of the young women, but Manuel could still visualize her face as he stared at her.

Manuel still had not opened up to Abby about his feelings. He was waiting for the perfect opportunity to bring it up. He was lost in his head, making up perfect scenarios to broach the subject, when someone tapped him on his shoulders. He turned around and found his bruder leaning in towards him.

"What is it?" he whispered.

"Father asked that you stop staring at the ladies and focus on the sermon," Samuel whispered back.

Manuel was embarrassed. He didn't realize that his father had noticed that his attention was divided. He slowly and carefully turned his head to glance at his father, and the old man gently motioned at him to adjust his attention.

Shortly after, the preacher finished his sermon and walked down the stand. After the closing hymn was sung, Herr Wheeler went up to the stand and addressed the congregation.

"We have an announcement to share with you all. As you all know, the Christmas celebration is just nine days away from today. We hope that every household present has set preparations in place for the celebration. Our assembly heads have unanimously agreed that this year's gathering will hold at the household of Herr

Gaius. We urge everyone to cooperate with the arrangements and work together so we can all enjoy and celebrate Gott for the blessing he hath given to us."

The congregants nodded in approval and the service was finally declared over. They all began to troop out of the barn in a file.

Outside, women and men gathered in small groups discussing in low chatters. The youngsters ran around excitedly, sharing their Christmas plans with their friends. A few who were in a hurry made their way to their horse-drawn buggies parked outside and went home.

"Manuel, we are very happy to see you back in the fold with us," Herr Wheeler said to Manuel as the two stepped out of the building.

"I'm delighted to be back, Sir. All my time away, I have always longed for the spirit of fellowship among my family and friends."

"How is your uncle?"

"He's doing quite well, Sir. He sent his regards to everyone down here."

"It's a pleasure to hear. Gott be praised. I hope you are staying until the Christmas celebrations are over?" Herr Wheeler asked.

"Yes, sir. I may even spend little time here if things work out as planned," he responded.

"That's good to hear," the older man said as he extended his hands and the two men shook.

Manuel looked over to where a few of his friends were gathered.

"Manny!" they called out to him to join them.

When he walked over, the young men exchanged greetings. These were the boys he grew up with as a child.

"Manny, it's good to see you again. It's been like forever," Aaron said as he patted Manuel on his back.

"Seems like the town did a whole lot of good for him. He's grown taller and broader than the rest of us," another boy teased and they all laughed.

"So how long will you be spending with us?" Jared asked.

"Until the Christmas celebrations are over. Probably up until the new year."

"Guess we'll find some time to hang around then, won't we?"

"Sure."

Abigail crept up to where Manuel stood with the lads and tapped him on the shoulder. He swerved around almost immediately.

"Hey, Abby."

"Hello, Manny. How was the service today?"

"It was quite remarkable. I so much missed the fellowship at your home," he said as a smile curved out of his mouth.

"That's great to hear."

"Do you have any plans for today?"

"Well, apart from the chores at home, I'll be spending the evening sewing my dress for the Christmas season. My sisters and I already have it scheduled."

"I had hoped we would find the opportunity to spend some time over at my house. We'll be having a game of ping-pong later this night. I would drop you off before it's too dark."

"Oh. I wish that were possible, but my sisters would be greatly disheartened, and I would hate to let them down," Abigail said, giving him a sympathetic look.

"Well, it's alright. But how about tomorrow? I'm free, and I could come help you out at work. What do you think?" he pressed.

"I would appreciate that," Abigail consented. She wouldn't mind some free labor at the workshop. At least, it would help her finish on time and have extra time on her hands to sort out some Christmas preparations.

"See you tomorrow then."

"See you too. Goodbye." Abigail waved as she proceeded toward the wagon where her bruder and sisters were waiting.

Abigail climbed into the horse, and her sisters began to tease.

"Abby, he's so sweet and handsome. Did he ask you out? Will you two court?"

As they ended their statements, they snickered.

Abby shook her head. "Stop it, girls. Manny is just a friend. He would never see me that way. Besides, he's not looking for a relationship. We are just hanging out and chatting like old-time friends. He's also assisting me at the workshop."

"Oh. Don't be naive, Abby. He's so in love with you. Never say never. I'm almost certain he will ask you to court."

"Manny will be moving back to his uncle after Christmas. So don't think you're getting rid of me so easily. He probably has someone over there, and I will find someone over here too. Soon." Abigail pointed at her sisters as though she were warning them off.

This cracked up the girls, but they kept teasing and wouldn't stop talking about Manuel.

"So, when are we going to meet to start working on our dresses?" Abigail interrupted them.

"How about this Friday?" said Debbie.

"Why don't you ask Manuel to take us into town to get some supplies, Abby?" Joanna chipped in suggestively.

Abigail shot her a piercing gaze.

"I don't mean any harm. It would just be nice to have him take us on a little ride into town. He knows the terrain better, don't you think?" Joanna asked, begging Debbie to say something.

"I think Joanna's right. Come on, it would be fun."

Abigail thought it over in her head, and then she said, "Father would never agree to that."

"We will convince him. Just leave the talking to me."

"Besides, one buggy would not be enough. We still need additional wagons and horses," Abigail protested, attempting every tactic to beg out of the situation.

"You speak as though that was a problem. Our dear bruder Jared will join us on the trip. Won't you, Jared?" Joanna leaned forward toward Jared, steering the horse through the snow-piled driveway in silence throughout their conversation.

Jared gestured reluctantly.

"Oh, come on, bruder. I promise to make a special present just for you. I'm doing this for Abigail. Help me out."

They all giggled at the mention of Abby.

"Alright. I'm in."

The girls cheered and soon launched arrangements on how they would proceed. They promised to invite some other girls into the group so they could all go together.

The following day, Manuel took his time to prepare for his meeting with Abigail at the workshop. His mamm would not let him help at home, insisting he needed all the time he could to rest and just relax. Hence, he had little or nothing to do around the house.

He had just finished dressing and put on a pair of winter boots and a woolen coat. He took out his gloves and ran down the stairs to meet his mamm in the kitchen. The smell of the morning breakfast filled the air.

"Good morning, mama."

His mamm turned around to take a good look at him. "Good morning, Manny. How was your night?" she asked.

"Better than ever."

Manuel seemed very excited and eager, and his mamm shot him a suspicious look. "What is the smile about this morning? What are you up to?" his mamm quizzed.

"Nothing, Mamm. What would you like me to assist with?"

"Well, if you insist, make some coffee for everyone. The kettle is over there," she said, directing him towards the large boiling kettle on the fire.

Manuel went over and fixed cups of coffee.

Soon, the family was all seated, and they had breakfast amidst small talk and plans about their day.

"Father," Adah began. "We would like to go into town this Friday to get some supplies for our presents. Some of the girls made arrangements, and we would like to join them."

Their father considered this for a while. It was the Christmas holidays, and he wanted them to have the best observance of it. But, at the same time, he wouldn't want his girls to be exposed to influence by outside traditions of Christmas.

"You do understand what the Christmas holiday is about for us, don't you?"

"Yes, father. We intend to buy—"

"Then that is not a problem as long as your bruder would be the one to drive you there."

The girls turned to look at Manny.

"Of course. I will take the girls into town," Manuel agreed, seeing that as an opportunity to take Abby into town as well.

After breakfast, Manny stayed behind to assist his siblings with chores around the home while their mamm prepared hot water bottles for everyone going out. The bottles would help keep them warm against the heavy winter storm.

After the chores were done, Manny put his gloves on and proceeded out the door.

"Aren't you forgetting something?" his mamm called out from behind him.

"What could that be?" He turned around to face her.

His mamm spread her arms out in front of her. Manny chuckled as he walked back for a hug.

His mamm held him right for a few seconds. "Be careful out there and try not to go where the snow is too deep for the horses, alright?" she cautioned.

"Mamm, I am not ten. I know what to do," he laughed at her overprotective manner.

"And make sure to shod the horses' feet with some winter shoes."

"Okay, mamm. I will do just that," he finally conceded and began to walk towards the door.

"Wait," his mamm said.

"Mamm!" Manuel whined and turned around to find her standing with a bottle in her hand.

"Take this with you for warmth when the weather gets worse, okay, and come back in time for lunch, will you?"

"Denke, mamm. I will," Manuel replied with a smile as he finally walked out of the door towards the driveway where the horse and wagon were stationed.

By the time Manuel got to the workshop, Abigail had already arrived and was about to boil the pears.

"Sorry I'm late. My mamm needed me. Why don't you let me help you with that?"

he said as he walked towards the fireplace, jacked the large steel pot up, and placed it on the fire.

"Denke," Abby whispered. "I see you're perfectly dressed for the weather," she added.

"Well, my mamm made sure of that."

Abigail chuckled. "Your mamm is a very kind woman. What would you do without her?" she taunted.

They sat together on the bench while waiting for the pears to boil. Outside, clumps of snow fell from the trees and scattered in the breeze, leaving sparkling showers in their wake. The bare branches of the trees creaked and clacked in the cold breeze.

"I miss those times when we used to run in the snow, build snowmen, and have fun snowball battles," she said, smiling longingly at the memories of their past.

"Well, who says we still can't have a shot at it? Come on, it will be fun." He got up instantly and held out his hands.

"No," Abby objected, laughing at how ridiculous they would look, two adults running around in the snow.

"Please!" Manny insisted with his hand still stretched out towards her.

Abigail considered for a moment and then said, "Alright."

She folded the cloak she had used to wrap around herself. Manny helped her into her coat, and they strode outside.

Manny walked over to the wagon and picked out a double pair of snow sleds. Abigail beamed with a smile from where she stood. He beckoned her to join him. As

Abby neared him, she stumbled and staggered into him. His arms closed around her and kept her upright, saving her from falling over into the snow. She looked up into his eyes and could have sworn she saw a slow smile curve his lips. His heart skittered wildly in an instant before she regained her stability and shuffled away from him.

Manuel could sense her embarrassment as her cheeks reddened but tried not to further aggravate her by talking about it. He, however, wondered if that meant she had some feelings towards him too. He hoped she did.

Holding Abby's hands to steady her, Manuel helped her onto her sled as he stepped onto his. He could see her legs wobbling as she sat.

"I haven't tried this in a very long time, Manny," Abigail protested as the sled began down the slope.

Manuel caught her arms just in time and pulled her to a stop. He steadied her with one hand while propelling his sled with his feet. They both began down the slope. The cold bit hard on his face and made his eyes water. He turned around to look at Abigail and found her wearing a bright dimpled smile on her face. This made him relax, and they went even faster, laughing and screaming as they slid to a stop.

"That was amazing. I enjoyed the ride," Abigail giggled. "It's been such a long time since I did something like this."

"Oh, I knew you would love it, of course. That's why I suggested it," Manuel grinned.

Abby molded a snowball and threw it at him. "Take that," she said and began to run towards the workshop.

Manuel laughed as he wiped the back of his head where the snowball landed. He proceeded to mold some of his own and aimed at her. Abby shrieked and ran even faster. The snowball missed her by inches, and she could feel the cold swoosh past her ears. Manny ran after her and tried again, and this time, it landed on her back.

"Yes!" He cheered as he celebrated his win while they both fell on the snow laughing.

"The pears!" Manuel gasped as he remembered. They both got up immediately, running as fast as their feet could carry them even as the snow slowed their movements.

When they got into the workshop, Abby used a large wooden spatula to check the pot and discovered that it had begun to burn. Her lips thinned out in disappointment. Manny felt terrible already. He reached toward her and put a hand on her shoulders.

"I'm sorry. We should not have gone off while this was on the fire."

"Oh, no. It's not your fault," Abigail objected. "This happens some of the times."

"Well, it probably wouldn't have happened this time if we had stayed put."

"I promise, it's not your fault. It would have happened either way if it's meant to. Besides, we were not gone for too long. I guess the fire was just a bit too much. I added more wood than normal."

Despite everything she tried to say to lessen his guilt, Manny would not stop blaming himself for what happened. He believed it could have been prevented if he had not distracted her with his snowplay.

"How can I make it up to you?"

"No," she shook her head.

"Please, I insist."

"Alright. You just might have the perfect opportunity to make it up to me. My friends and I would be going into town on Friday to get supplies to make some homemade gifts. They were hoping you would drive us."

"Really?"

Abby responded with a nod.

"Yes! My answer is Yes. What time will we be leaving?"

"Now slow down, Manny. I'll get back to you on that." Abby laughed at his eagerness.

"Well, what do we do with these pears?"

"We'll just scoop the usable portion and use it to process the butter. The rest of it will be discarded. The portion will just be smaller."

"Won't it affect the taste of the butter?" Manuel wanted to know.

"No, not at all. Don't worry. I'll have you taste it when it's done. I brought some biscuits and toast for lunch."

"Oh. That reminds me. I promised my mamm I would be back for lunch."

Abigail's countenance changed as he mentioned leaving. Her face became a little sad.

"You'll be leaving soon then," she said, trying not to show her despair.

Manuel sensed a change in her tone and expression and smiled. She wanted him to stay. He was more than happy to put off returning home for a little longer. His mamm would understand. Spending time in Abby's company was an absolute pleasure for him. He would not miss the opportunity for anything.

As they worked on the butter, Manuel decided that this might be the right time to express his intentions. Abby's willingness to have him with her indicated that she may share the same feelings towards him. However, he didn't know how to broach the subject. He was still fearful of being rejected by her.

Finally, Manuel said, "Abby, I was planning to buy land here in town and maybe build a house." He wore a serious expression on his face.

"Really? Are you planning to move back here?"

"I've been considering it for about a year now. I think it's time for me to settle down now among my people and maybe start a family."

Abigail's heart skipped a bit at the mention of a family. She was silent for so long that Manuel started to think it was a mistake to have made the move. But then, she said, "Have you found someone?"

Manuel hesitated.

"I think I may have, but I don't know how to approach her about it. I'm unsure if she feels the same way about me."

"Then you should ask her."

"You think?"

"Yes. Totally. Ask her. She just might feel the same way about you."

Manuel sighed, uncertain if she knew he was referring to her and encouraging him, or if she frankly believed he was talking about someone else.

"Where did you two meet? Does she live in town too? Do you think she'll come down with you here?" Abby threw a barrage of questions at him, eager to know more about his love interest.

Manuel braced himself.

"No. She is not in town. We've been long-time friends, and I know she would love to live here."

"Is she someone I might know?" she asked, a bit more serious now.

"Probably."

Abigail felt Manuel's hesitation to reveal who his love interest was, so she decided to drop the subject. She didn't want to pressure him to admit it until he was comfortable enough to share it. She hoped it was one of their good friends.

"Well, I hope the best for you. Just don't forget to tell me when the wedding bells ring," she joked.

Manuel smiled, a bit unhappy that he was unable to confess his feelings before her.

By now, they had finished processing the butter. While Abigail scooped them into air-tight jars, Manuel discarded the burnt portion of the pears. He promised himself to supply her with a fresh batch of pears from his uncle's orchard to make up for the lost ones.

When Manuel returned, he found Abby sitting on the bench with a serving of butter, some biscuits, and toast, just as she promised. She motioned at him to join her.

"I've been waiting for you. Come sit. What took you so long?"

"I stopped by to check on the horse and fed her some hay."

"Alright. Let's eat."

Manuel sat down on the other end of the bench. Abigail asked him to say a prayer over the meal. He was impressed and could not stop imagining how it would be if they were both married and living together, sitting down at the table like this for meals, with their little ones running around the house.

Abigail took some toast, spread it generously with some butter, and handed it to Manuel. He took a bite and moaned in pleasure. Abigail couldn't help but beam up with a smile.

"Tastes as good as the first time," he said. "You really are gifted at this. The taste is unique. It is sweet and savory at the same time."

"Denke," Abigail said and proceeded to pour a cup of tea for him and herself.

"Are you courting someone?" Manual asked after a while.

"No," Abigail answered, wondering why he was suddenly interested in her relationship life.

Manual could not believe her.

"Why?"

"I just haven't found the right one yet."

"Really? So how would you know the right one if you met him," he quizzed.

"He must be a very kind gentleman. Kindness is a strong quality to me. A kind spouse considers his frau's feelings and strives to win her affections."

"Hmm. That is true."

"I know."

"So, are you saying that you haven't met one man in the whole of Hickland valley who is kind in that way?"

"Oh, stop it. That's not what I said. I just haven't found or perhaps met the one for me."

"Can I ask a question? I need an honest answer."

"Okay."

"You've known me for a long time. You've seen me through childhood and now as an adult man these past few days. Would you describe me as a kind man?"

Abigail turned the question over in her mind. She needed to choose her words carefully.

"I would say yes. You weren't one of those mischievous boys back in school. You've always been kind and disciplined, and even now, as an adult, you've been very sweet and helpful. I have benefited wholly from that kindness, so my answer is yes."

Manuel's face warmed up with a smile. He was comforted with the knowledge that Abigail thought highly of him.

"Denke," he mouthed.

Abigail grinned at him, patting his shoulder softly.

After eating, they loaded the batch of butter jars into the wagon. Abigail got in the back while Manny climbed up the driver's seat and pulled the horse's harness, and the animal began trotting in the direction of home. The snow had stopped falling by now. Only a thick layer of powdery fresh snow carpeted the ground.

It wasn't very easy moving along the terrain. Abigail pulled the wagon blanket over herself, her hot water bottle underneath her clothing. On the side of the roads, children were kicking up clouds of fresh snow that had just fallen. Others were making snowmen across the hedges. Abigail smiled to herself as she stared at them.

"Denke for today. You made everything so much easier for me."

"I had a wonderful time," he said, smiling over at her.

The horse finally pulled up in front of Abigail's home. Manuel got down and tied the horse to a tree, then began to carry the butter jars into the house. Abigail ran ahead of him to hold the door open. Her mamm stepped onto the porch as Abigail opened the door.

"Good day, Mrs. Wheeler," Manuel greeted as Abigail's mamm approached.

"Manny, it's good to see you again. Welcome, son. How is your mamm? Do tell her I will visit tomorrow to discuss our plans for Christmas. That reminds me, I still owe you a meal for the last time you came here," she said.

"Mamm's fine. I'll pass on the message. And you don't need to worry. Abigail and I have eaten lunch already. Abby, right?" he said, turning to her.

Abigail nodded in agreement.

"Just add my treat to the Christmas meals," he said.

"Alright then. I will make you my special whoopie pie for Christmas. But still, I can't let you leave empty-handed." She dashed into the house, reappearing a few seconds later with a small fruit basket. "Take this for now."

Manuel accepted the gift and thanked her. Then, he said goodbye to the two women and left.

Abigail stood on the porch, watching Manuel as he made his way towards the buggy. He effortlessly maneuvered his way through the snow, his broad shoulders flexing under his shirt. A warm feeling rushed through her body again.

Manuel affected her, Abigail realized. She was starting to see him a bit differently from how she had seen him as a child. Her mind was stirred back to reality when she noticed he was waving at her from the wagon. She waved back and walked into the house, saddened by the knowledge that he had someone already. Someone he intended to settle down with soon, probably one of their friends. A bit of jealous feeling made its way into her heart.

Over the next few days, Manuel was very handy around the Wheeler house. Apart from helping Abigail run errands and make deliveries throughout the county, he also helped to repair the front fence. He took advantage of every opportunity to spend as much time as he could with Abigail, hoping it would endear him to her.

This was one of the reasons why when Jared mentioned that their barn roof had suffered some leakages, Manuel quickly offered to help with the repairs. The following day, he headed happily to the Wheeler house. On getting there, he met with Herr Wheeler.

"Good morning, sir," he greeted.

"Good morning, Manuel. How are you, son?"

"I'm fine, sir. Is Jared home? He spoke of a leakage in your barn he needed assistance with, and in the spirit of Christmas, I have come with some tools to fix it," he said while rummaging through his toolbox.

"That's very generous of you," Mr. Wheeler said, impressed by Manuel's willingness to help. "May Gott bless your soul."

Manual and Jared worked on the barn roof until late midday when Mrs. Wheeler came out and invited the boys in for lunch.

Chapter Four

Early Friday morning, Manuel was out brushing the horse and polishing the wagon. He had made up his mind to confess his feelings for Abigail. He was going to tell her on her way back from the market later that day, then he'd use the opportunity to invite her to the Sing for a date.

Manuel thought of what he could get Abigail for Christmas. He needed something special, yet simple. A gift that would serve as an expression of his love for her. Then he remembered he still owed her some pears. He needed to ride into town and get them. He would surprise her with them at the Sing that Sunday.

By noon, the women were ready for the trip to the farmers' market. Adah and Jael and their mamm, along with Mrs. Wheeler, Abigail, Debbie, and Joanna, were all going. Jared and Manuel drove them in the double wagons. While the women shopped for vegetables and dessert ingredients, Manuel went down into town to get the pears. He stuffed them in the back buggy where it would not be easily seen. Then, he joined the company of others, looking for a suitable present for Abigail.

Abigail was choosing some greens at a stall when Manuel approached from behind her. "Hey, Abby."

She turned around to see him standing there smiling.

"Hello, Manny,"

"How's the shopping going?"

"Well, we've gotten most of the vegetables and baking flour with ingredients. I just needed to pick some greens before we leave,"

"Where's everyone else?"

"I'm guessing they're all done. They should be outside by the wagon. Jared is loading up the trucks with the goods."

"Alright, let's hurry up then," he said as he reached for her basket.

Abigail noticed that one of his hands was hidden behind his back.

"What have you got there?" she quizzed, looking at him suspiciously while trying to see behind him. Manuel brought out his hand, revealing a single rose.

"I got this for you," he said as he held up the flower to her.

"Really? Why?" Abigail muttered before she could stop herself. She hadn't seen that coming. Roses are an expression of love, and she wondered why Manuel would be giving her one.

"Abby, I-I."

"What?" Abigail stared at him in confusion.

"Look, Abby. Would you go to the Sing with me?"

"Manuel? I do not understand you. Last week you told me you had someone, and now you're asking me out? What's going on?" Abigail quizzed, waiting for an explanation.

Manuel did not know how to explain himself. So he just stood there, unable to find his voice while Abigail turned and walked away.

Manual was very gloomy on the ride back home. His sister had witnessed the incident at the stall and had reported it to their mamm. His mamm had waited until they got home to broach the subject.

"Are you alright, son?" she asked, giving him a sympathetic look.

"I'm fine, Ma," he replied, looking anything but fine.

His mamm pulled him by the arm and was about to press on but then decided against it. She didn't want to pressure him or aggravate his gloomy disposition.

***

Abigail's mamm noticed how her countenance had changed when she walked from the stalls to the buggy. She tried to find out what went wrong, but Abigail would not say. Instead, the young lady kept insisting that all was fine.

Abigail could not understand Manuel's sudden interest in her. Just days ago, he had told her he had someone he intended to settle with. Was he simply trying to toy with her? She had thought better of him than that. He came off as a responsible young man, and she couldn't understand why he would go around trying to court more than one girl at a time.

Later that night, Abigail approached her mamm. She needed someone to share the matter weighing on her mind.

"Mamm," she said. Her mamm sat on the rocking chair, knitting a pair of gloves she planned to gift the younger children.

Her mamm looked up from her knitting. "Abbie? Is there a problem?"

"I'm sorry about how I acted earlier in the day," Abigail apologized.

"It's alright. Is there something you'd like to share?"

Abigail fell at her mamm's feet, causing the ball of yarn to tumble off.

"Mamm, I'm confused. I would like to hear your opinion on something."

"What is it, child?" her mamm asked, putting the half-knitted gloves down to give her all her attention.

"It's about Manuel. We have been spending time together since his return, with him helping me out at the workshop. He informed me that he intended to settle down soon and that he had someone whom he planned to marry. But today at the market, he came up to me with a rose, asking me out to the Sing. I'm really confused. I feel like he's trying to mess with me."

Her mamm sighed. "Abby, did he tell you who it was he intended to marry?"

"No."

"What were his exact words? Can you remember?"

"Yes. He said there was someone, but he hadn't told her yet. He was waiting for the right time."

There was silence between mamm and dochder for some wee seconds.

"Is it possible that he was referring to you when he said so?"

It was then it hit Abigail. Her mamm may be right. Manual had said he didn't know how to approach his love interest. She thought he was confiding in her as a friend.

But, perhaps, it was her whom he was interested in.

"Do you like him?" her mamm asked, interrupting her thoughts.

"I think I do. I have been thinking about him a little too much lately," Abigail said, hiding her face in her mamm's skirt.

"Then I think you should allow him to explain himself."

"Okay. Denke, mama."

Abigail felt more at ease after speaking with her mamm. She was going to attend the Sing tomorrow in hopes that Manuel would show up.

***

Manuel was miserable the whole evening. He did not come down for dinner with the family as usual until Adah went up to call him. At the table, he kept fidgeting with his cutlery. No one said anything as they were now all aware of the cold rejection he had gotten from Abigail.

After dinner, Manuel's father asked to have a word with him.

"How was your day today?" his father asked, trying to start the conversation. "I noticed you were picking at your meals during dinner time."

"I wasn't very hungry, daed."

"Manuel. I have seen you around this house for the past few days you've been home; today has been quite different. If there's anything I can do about what is upsetting you, please let me know whenever you feel okay to share."

"Yes, Father," Manuel said and thanked his father. He could not bring himself to divulge what caused him so much despair.

The next day, Saturday, Manuel and his father spent the day setting up the barn where the Christmas dinner would be held. They raised a stage where the young children would sing Christmas hymns. Manuel could not keep his mind off the incident of the previous day. Thinking about it made him squirm. He wanted to forget it so badly, but it kept nudging at him. Manuel thought it would be best to get the advice of someone older, someone like his father.

So, around noon when the two men stopped to eat lunch, Manuel decided to speak to his father.

"Father? About yesterday, I would like to hear your thoughts on something that has worried my mind."

His father was pleased to see that he was ready to open up.

"Let's sit then," his father said, leading the way to a bench in the room.

"What is it, son?" he asked after they had both sat down.

"There is someone I may be interested in courting, but I think I may have messed it up already and probably ruined what was a beautiful friendship. She turned down my proposal, and I don't think she wants to have anything to do with me again."

"Hmm!" his father sighed. "How exactly did you mess it up, son?"

"I may have given her the impression that I had someone else of interest. I was afraid of being too direct, but now, it turned out to be a disaster. She totally misunderstood. It was her whom I was referring to."

"Have you taken out the time to explain this to her?" his father enquired.

"No. I haven't had the chance. I intended to take her to the Sing at Herr Daniel's home tomorrow evening. But I can't see how I can do that as it is."

"I would advise you to attend the Sing still. She may be there. Approach her and ask for a chance to explain yourself properly. Then, hopefully, she'll come around."

Manuel thought his father was right.

"You can take a gift offering with you, something of value to her. It is a good way of reaching a woman's heart," his father added with a knowing smile.

Manuel suddenly remembered the pears he had brought home for Abigail. He had wrapped them in paper boxes and stored them in a cold root cellar to preserve them. They were the perfect peace offering, and he decided he would take them to the Sing.

"Denke so much, Father. I will do just as you have said."

"You're welcome, my son. I commend you for sharing. It was an honorable thing to do. Never shy away from sharing your problems, especially with family. It is said, a problem shared is a problem half solved. You have grown into a fine young man, and I'm proud of you."

Manuel chuckled at that, although he knew his father was right. He felt a lot better almost immediately. It seemed like a heavy load had been lifted off his chest. He also felt contentment in knowing his father thought highly of him. It was proof that he was on the right track.

Chapter Five

Manuel was too excited to sleep. He spent the night counting the minutes and hours until daybreak. Early Sunday morning, he was up at the first sign of dawn, humming old Christmas tunes while doing the chores.

By the time the rest of the household awoke, Manuel stood in the kitchen making scrambled eggs and toast for breakfast.

"Good morning," he greeted each of them as they walked into the kitchen, awed by his transformation from gloomy to gleeful.

"Take a seat, everyone. I will be in charge of kitchen duties this morning, so sit back, relax and enjoy," he announced as his siblings chattered excitedly. "This morning, we are going to have the Manny's special," he said as he served eggs and toast on everyone's plates.

Voices of laughter filled the whole room.

"Scrambled eggs? Manny's special?" Adah cried out, laughing.

After they had breakfast and finished the rest of the chores, the family sat together to read the Bible in German and share their thoughts on the scriptures, as was their custom on Sundays.

Later, when it started to snow outside, the younger children went out to play on the driveway, catching snowflakes with their tongues and building snowmen while their parents sat on the porch, playing a board game, watching them have fun.

As the evening approached, Manuel got up to prepare for the Sing. He would drive with his sisters, Adah and Jael, there.

"Adah, are you ready yet?" he called out from his room.

"Almost done," the girls echoed.

"Hurry up, girls, okay?"

Manuel was too excited and had spent the whole afternoon planning how he would approach Abigail and get things running smoothly between them.

Before the singing, usually, someone would start a game of volleyball. One was just getting started when Manuel and his sisters arrived, and he was pleased. He was good at volleyball and hoped Abigail would get to see him score. Quickly, Manuel hurried over and joined in the game.

He did well, scoring three times for his team, and everyone cheered when his team won, even the losing team.

When the game was over, everyone trooped into the large barn to begin the singing proper. The boys and girls sat on opposite sides of the benches, and songs were chosen from the old hymn book.

Manuel scanned the room, trying to see where Abigail was. He had played against her brother Jared during the game, so there was a possibility that Abigail was here, too. He wondered if she was still mad at him. Whatever the case, he was here to explain things and make them right.

The rhythmic voices of the singers cascaded through the room. Finally, after a few songs, it was time for a break. Drinks and snacks were brought out in large trays, and everyone helped themselves to them.

Manuel had begun to grow anxious. He still couldn't see Abigail. He finally got up to find her but found her sister, Debbie, instead.

"Hello, Debbie," he called out to her.

"Hi, Manuel. It's nice to see you around,"

"Denke. Is Abigail here with you?"

"Yes. She's over there," Debbie replied, pointing towards the barn exit and excusing herself, running off immediately to meet with friends.

Manuel looked in the direction and caught sight of Abigail walking toward him. She appeared to be smiling at him. Just then, he remembered the pears in the back of his wagon that he intended to present as a peace offering to her, just as his father had advised him.

He immediately ran out of the barn to get them.

***

Abigail had watched Manuel with admiration while he played volleyball outside in the snow. She was happy to see him at the Sing because it would allow her to talk things over and accept a ride home, to show that she consented to his proposal.

After they had dispersed to snack and drink, she looked for him among the crowd before she saw him with her sister. But as she walked up towards him, Manuel turned around immediately and fled the room.

Abigail was stunned. She felt her face burn and her eyes sting from the tears fighting to fall. She had never felt this embarrassed in her life. She could not understand why Manuel was sending her mixed signals. None of it made sense. Maybe her mamm was wrong after all. Manuel was playing a game, and she was unwilling to be part of any of it. With those thoughts, she stormed out of the barn house.

By the time Manuel returned to the room, Abigail was nowhere to be found. The crowd had also begun to thin by now. Most of the young men and women had departed the Sing while a few still hung around in pairs. It was the second time Manuel had had his heart crushed.

"How did it go, son?" his mamm asked when Manuel walked into the house.

"She didn't show up, mamm," he lied, trying not to get into the conversation, but the look on his face betrayed him. He took the pears back to the root cellar. He didn't even care about them anymore. Immediately after Christmas, he would return to his uncle's farm.

"What happened?" his mamm asked the girls who came in behind him.

They all shook their heads.

"I saw Abigail run out the door, looking very upset, mamm. I doubt they got the chance to resolve the misunderstanding," Jael said.

She sighed. She would have to step in, she decided.

Monday morning, when preparations were in full swing, Manuel's mamm and

Abigail's mamm sat together. The younger children were in the barn, rehearsing for their parts in the Christmas play. Their melodious voices could be heard from all corners of the home.

"Have you noticed the tension between our children?" Frau Wheeler asked

Frau Zook nodded. "It's something we need to address. They both seem to be in love but struggle to navigate the relationship."

"Why don't we intervene? I mean, not outrightly, but let's steer them in the right direction. What do you think?"

"What do you have in mind?" Manuel's mamm asked. Frau Wheeler leaned in and whispered something to her. The two women nodded in agreement, putting their plan together.

The Christmas morning began with singing hymns, prayers, and reading the scriptures in Manuel's home. It was the same as always since they were younger. Their father would lead the morning devotion and prayer, giving thanks for the gift of life and family.

After the session, the children immediately took up their assigned chores before other members of the groups arrived. Manual looked up the chore board. His task was to make a quick trip to the market to get some sweet peppers.

Manual got into the buggy and set out to the market. He wandered through the stalls, looking for the particular type his mamm had asked for. Finally, after he had searched for a while without luck, he decided to ask for help. The woman pointed him in the direction of the far aisle.

"Merry Christmas and denke," he waved as he rushed toward the aisle.

"Merry Christmas," she greeted in response.

Manual stopped suddenly when he recognized the young woman standing at the stall, bargaining with the buyer. It was Abigail. He felt dreadful and considered walking off in the opposite direction, but on second thought, he decided to approach.

"Good morning," he greeted the store manager.

Abigail whirled around in surprise.

What was he doing here?

"Hello, Abby," she heard him say.

"Hi, Manuel."

"Merry Christmas."

"Merry Christmas to you too," Abigail responded. Then, with a puzzled look, she asked, "What are you doing here?"

"My mamm sent me here to buy some sweet peppers."

Abigail's eyes widened in surprise.

"Really? My mamm sent me here to buy the same thing."

It was Manuel's turn now to be surprised. This was no coincidence. Their mamms had sent them off to the same place, not necessarily for some sweet peppers but so they would meet. When they realized what was happening, they started laughing.

"I think we have been set up," Abigail said.

"Did you, by any chance, talk to your parents about us?"

Abigail nodded sheepishly.

"Well, I did too. I believe they noticed the friction between us."

"I'm sorry about the other day at the farmers' market. I should have given you the chance to explain yourself," Abigail apologized, beating him to it.

"No, I should be the one to apologize, Abby. I should have been forward with you from the first day, but I was too afraid that you would reject my proposal. So now I know better to just ask."

"But what happened that night at the Sing? You turned around and left immediately when you saw me."

"I now understand how it looked, but I had forgotten the pears I promised and had run back to the wagon to get them. It was intended as a peace offering."

"Really?" Abigail groaned, laughing at herself for thinking he was trying to avoid her. "My Gott, I had thought the worst of you. I'm so sorry."

"It's alright. I felt equally heartbroken when I came back and you were nowhere to be found."

They paid for the peppers—just in case their mamms did need them. As they walked back through the market, Manuel shared with Abigail his decision about the land he had planned to purchase.

"Would you like to help me find the most suitable one?" he asked, turning to her with a smile.

"It would be an honor," Abigail said as color began to rise on her cheeks.

The weather outside was perfect as they strode out towards the buggy. Manual reached into the back and brought out a box.

"I got something for you," he said, placing the box into her hands.

Abigail opened it up. It was a wooden recipe box card containing varieties of butter-making instructions.

"This is a really thoughtful gift, Manuel. Denke very much."

Manual nodded. He was thrilled that she loved it, but even more thrilled that she had agreed to allow him to court her.

"I'm sorry I didn't get you something."

"You did. You're my perfect Christmas gift."

Abigail glowed as she stepped in for a hug.

By the time they got home, guests were trooping into the house, with buggies lined up in the streets. Manual and Abigail walked in, hand in hand, through the doors. The scents of vanilla candles flickering in the room wafted through the air. There were lots of chatters, smiles, and laughter filling the room.

It was going to be the best Christmas ever.

The End

FREE GIFT

Just to say thanks for checking our works we like to gift you

Our Exclusive Never Before Released Books

100% FREE!

Please GO TO

http://cleanromancepublishing.com/gift

And get your FREE gift

Thanks for being such a wonderful client.

Please Check out My Other Works

By checking out the link below

http://cleanromancepublishing.com/rbauth

Thank You

Many thanks for taking the time to buy and read through this book.

It means lots to be supported by SPECIAL readers like YOU.

Hope you enjoyed the book; please support my writing by leaving an honest review to assist other readers.

.

With Regards,

Ruth Bawell